THE CRUEL REVENGE

REVENGE THAT LEADS TO A SERIAL KILLER

SONIA MARANDI

I thank my good friend whom I call Winston! Thanks to him, because of him, I was able to make this story. Winston is an inspiration, he allowed me to make a character about him, he is the most generous, kind, and sweetest person I know. He helped me on my bad days, and I would like to repay him by thanking him a lot! Thank You, Winston, I hope everyone meets people like you... The Winston character in the story is based on my friend! Thanks to him. He also gave me a story idea which was the best! Thanks a lot, my friend...

Contents

Foreword

My goal is to entertain you all, show my creativity by writing books. Many people like other types of stories but I like Thriller, suspicious, crime stories. There are many stories I think I didn't know how to show to people so, I wrote stories which I like! and I hope you like my stories.

Acknowledgements

Message from the author: I want to thank him, who has helped me in making this book! special thanks to the editor, she has helped me so much! she made all this for you. And again I want to thank them so much for helping me in making this book. Not to forget my viewers who read and view my books...

CHAPTER I

6 People are missing

It was evening... it was raining, a boy ran towards the police station. "HELP! PLEASE HELP ME!" The boy said and started crying, "Child, what happened?" A police officcr *(Marie Sanders)* asked him. "My-My Family! Th-they were not there in the house!" The boy said and started to scream, "Calm down... what's your name?" Marie asked, "M-my name is *Winston Monet*" "Ok, Winston, can you tell what happened to your family?" Marie asked,

"Today, at 9 AM, I and my family went to our relative's house which is in the Jeps Med, we went from Kine Med, where my house is, to Jeps Med. We were returning home, suddenly my parents went another way so I followed them, but then, I lost my way... I was lost and couldn't find my parents, some big kids approached me and stole things from me. I walked and found myself in a village, the villagers tried to help me, they took me to Kine Med, it was already 5 PM. When we reached Kine Med, I saw my house and rushed to it, but when I opened the gate of my house, I saw bloodstains all over the house! No one was there in the house, I turned back around, the villagers also disappeared and one villager hasn't gone so he told me, 'go to the police station...' and some dust particles came into my eyes so I had to close my eyes, but when I opened my eyes, he was gone... But, as he told me to go to the police station, I came here"

" Do you think it is a murder?" Marie asked, "We need to check the house!" Another police officer (Martin Branson)

said. The police and Winton went to Kine Med, they examined the house and said, "We didn't find any bodies, we found samples of the bloodstains, the test will come tomorrow" Marie said, "Winston, where are you going to stay tonight?" Martin asked, "Martin! I heard you have an empty house nearby, so he can stay there!" Marie said, "Great Idea, Marie!" Martin replied, "Winston, are you okay with that? You can stay there until we finish this case" Marie asked, "Okay..." Winston said. Martin took Winston to the empty house near his house, "This house is empty, you can take some of my old blankets to sleep, lay down" Martin said and gave the blankets to Winston... The police went to Winston's relative's house, they were shocked after seeing the house, the condition of the house was as Winston's house, bloodstains all over the house... "Look like the relatives are also missing, I checked the house and it seems like, no one is there in the house..." Martin said, "Hmm... we also have to take this blood for a test!" Marie said, "Martin! Can you and a few other officers can go and enquire about his family and his relatives?" Marie asked Martin, "Sure!" Martin replied and went to his neighboring house with a few officers...Winston and Martin met again, "Hello buddy! How are you feeling here?" Martin asked, "Sir, I am feeling comfortable but... also worried," Winston said, Martin was surprised, "What happened? Why are you worried?" Martin asked, "Sir... it's been 1 month and my best friend is missing and no one has found her..." Winston said, "Oh, sorry to hear... Anyway, we will try to find her also, so what's her name?" Martin asked, "Julia Wilde" Winston replied, "Okay! So, Winston, we have come here to ask you a few questions" Martin said, "Okay" Winston replied, "Also, we have to say that... your relatives are also missing, in their house also, bloodstains were there all over the house, just like your house" Martin said, Winston was shocked, "Winston, do your family go outside?" Martin asked, "My father goes to work and wouldn't come home for days, my mother don't go outside, I and my young brother goes to play outside at the park," Winston said, Martin and his crew asked some other questions about Winston's family...

The next day; Marie called Winston to the police station, "What happened mam? Why did you call me here?" Winston asked, "We got the blood samples in your old house and your relatives' house," Marie said, "And they are *A positive and O positive, (From your old house)* Does anyone in your have these types of blood?" Marie asked, "Yes... A positive is my father's and brother's and O positive is my mother's" Winston replied, "Oh..." "So that means your family was... murdered?" Martin asked, but Winston went away to his house, he was depressed, "Is it true that all were murdered! But why?" Winston asked himself and went to take a nap.

CHAPTER II

My bestfriend is missing

While Winston was busy sleeping, he saw something in his dream, it was his best friend, Julia! "Winston! Winston! What happened? Why didn't you come to play, I was waiting for you..." Julia said, Winston woke up and went to the park, but he didn't see Julia, instead, he saw, Julia's elder sister, June. Winston went towards June and asked her, "Sister June, has Julia came today to play?" "Winston, have you forgotten that Julia is still missing..." June replied, Winston didn't say any words and went away, but before leaving, June said, "Winston! 1 month ago, Julia gave me this letter and told me to give it to you, I forgot to give you, so I am giving it now" June said, Winston took the letter and went back to his house... "Julia... you liar! It's not even a shocking thing for me... you always lied to me, Liar!" And Winston lied down to take nap, suddenly, he saw the letter which June gave him, "Oh yeah... this letter..." He said, and opened the letter,

"Winston... it's been 8 years, we know each other, don't know but it looks like I have feelings for you... What do you think? I think you would say, 'Julia... I knew it!' If you don't have feelings for me, that's okay, because we can become best friends!" Winston read the letter, he was surprised, "What! Julia, why didn't u tell me about this before..." Winston started to cry. And slept, "Wake up! Winston! It's 10 AM!" Julia said, "Julia... you are here? How?" Winston asked, "What are you even talking about? You didn't write the holiday Homework, that's why I came here, Now wake up, and complete your homework!" Julia said, *and smiled.* Suddenly, Winston woke up, "It was just a dream..." He said and went towards his bag, took some books, and started to complete his work, "This is what you wanted Julia? I will do it... I will write..." Winston said. After a few hours later, when Winston completed his work, he went to Julia's house, "Hello Winston, what happened? Came to meet Julia?" Julia's mother asked, "No aunt, Can you all help me in finding Julia, as it's 1 month and she is still missing..." Winston said, "Yeah... I was also thinking to find her," Julia's mother said, "Then let's go to the police station!" Julia's father said, "Winston, I heard your family is missing, what happened to them?" Julia's father asked Winston, "Don't know Uncle, I and the police are still finding them..." Winston replied. Julia's parents went to the police station, "Sir, it's been 1 month! My daughter is missing, please find her!" Julia's father said, "Sir, we are still finding her, please be patient," The police officer said. Meanwhile, Winston, went to Julia's neighbors' house, and asked about Julia, "Have you seen her?" Winston asked, but their reply were always, "No... we have not seen her..." Winston was worried, he went home disappointed, while he was going home, he saw many posters of the missing child; Julia...It was evening, and Martin also came back to his house, Winston went to his house and asked, "Sir! Have you found anything?" "Well, Winston, we didn't find anything, no bodies, no evidence. So, tomorrow we are going to paste some posters of your family, will you help us?" Martin replied, "Sure!" Winston replied, and went to his house... "Tomorrow I will ask my classmates about Julia!" Winston thought and slept.

The next day, Winston went to his school, he asked his teachers and classmates asked about Julia, but they always said, "No! I have not seen Julia!" Winston was still disappointed, suddenly, some children came to bully Winston, "I heard your 'best friend' is now missing, now what you are gonna do, orphan?" they said, Winston was still sad, so he didn't argue with them and went home quietly...

CHAPTER III

6 People are dead

Winston came home. Suddenly, Martin knocked on the door, "Winston! Come, we have to paste the posters!" He said, and Winston went with him... they pasted as many posters as they could. But, it was useless because no one saw them. A few weeks later, 6 corpses were found in the Las Med! And it was Winston's family... "*We can see, they were murdered!* Look! They were shot, by a pistol!" Marie said, "But how are the bodies here? They never went to Las Med!" Martin asked, "It's still a mystery, but now, we have to find the murderer!" Marie said. Martin went to Winston's house, "Winston... Sorry to tell but, your family was murdered and their corpses were found in Las Med!" He said, "What?! How is that possible? They never went to Las Med..." Winston said and started to cry... "All are dead! Mother, Father, Uncle, Aunt, my young brother, my cousin all are gone! All left me!" He sobbed, "Winston don't cry, we will find the murderer!" Martin said. Martin and his crew were busy inspecting the area where the bodies were found, suddenly, a police officer found something! "Sir! There are some bullets here!" He said Martin and the crew went to the place, Martin grabbed a bullet and looked closely, "These were used... and it is a Pistol Bullet! Marie was right! Now we can find the pistol from which it was shot!" Martin said, and they took the bullets..."Marie! I need your help! Can you find which pistol it is? We have some bullets" Martin said to Marie, "From which pistol they were shot? Should I find that?" Marie asked, "Yes!" Martin replied. Marie inspected the bullets and a few minutes later, she told, "I think these bullets are from the pistol; Astra 600! These bullets fit that pistol!"

"So, now we should find where the pistol got sold!" Martin said and everyone agreed to Martin, "Riffles, pistols, these are found in *Black Markets*! So we should find nearby black markets, probably we can find where Astra 600 is sold!" Martin said. They tried to find black markets and found a black market in Nas Led... "We are police, don't worry! We are not here to arrest you, we came here to ask some questions... "Is Astra 600 are sold here?" The officers asked, "Yes! I sell that pistol!" The seller replied, "Do you remember any person buying that pistol?" The police officer asked, "I remember the buyer... but he hid his face, I was not able to see him" The seller replied, "Did he mention his name? How does he look?" They asked, "Umm... I don't think he said his name. He wore a big coat, in a black color... he hid his face with a handkerchief" The seller said, "Okay..." The police officers said and went away... "It was useless going there!" Martin said. It was evening and everyone went to their home. Meanwhile, Winston ate his dinner and went to sleep, suddenly he remembered something... "4 years ago, when I was 10-years-old, my family went on a trip! My Uncle and his family also came, I still remember, Steven (Winston's cousin) was the most annoying on the trip, I can't believe Micheal (Winston's younger brother) was not annoying on that day! We went to the Kine Med Forest. That day was my best day! I, Steven, and Micheal we did a race and I won, we ate a lot of food, and the cookies were the best! We also discovered many plants and flowers, *Gnomeplant* was my favorite flower because it was pinkish-white which always reminds me of Julia! And the next day, I showed the flower to Julia, and she turned pinkish-white like the flower, we also took many pictures, and showed them to Julia and she was happy but jealous... On the trip, we were bored, and Micheal even slept! And so Steven. I was so bored, my cousin and brother also slept, I was not able to play with them, but it was a good trip and a great day! But... for a moment, I was scared, scared if I got lost or my any family member get lost... I never wanted that day. But, did I have an ill-luck? Now, they are no more with me... The 6 people were lost and then, they are dead. WHY? Why does it happen only with me?" Winston thought and slept.

The next day; *The Police found a corpse in a park of Jeps Med...*

• • •

CHAPTER IV

My bestfriend is dead?

"Whose corpse is this?" Marie asked, "NO WAY!! SHE IS-SHE IS JULIA!! THE MISSING GIRL!!" Martin replied. Marie was shocked, "Sh-she is Winston's best friend, right?" She asked, "Y-yes..." Martin said in a sad tone, "Is Julia... murdered?" Martin asked, "Y-yes..." Marie said, "But she was not shot by any pistol, she was stabbed by a knife!" Marie added, "What!?" All were surprised, Martin went to Winston's house and said, "Winston... I am very sorry to say, but your best friend, Julia... s-she, unfortunately, is dead..." Said in a sad tone and sobbed, "No! NO! THIS IS NOT TRUE!! JULIA WAS MISSING BECAUSE SHE WAS DEAD? NO!" Winston shouted and started to cry, "Sir Martin, this is not true right?" Winston asked, "It is true..." Martin said, "I don't believe it! I want to see her!" Winston said, "You could see only her corpse..." Martin said and took Winston with him to Julia's corpse. Winston saw Julia's corpse and he started to cry and went away to his house back, "I should have never gone there... It is true, she passed away. Julia, you were a good friend and no one should forget you, that's why I am thinking to do something for you..." Winston said to himself, then, he took a paper and a pen, and started writing a letter for Julia, a few minutes later, Winston finished writing the letter. In the letter, it was written;

"My dearest friend or my best friend... ever since we became friends, I didn't know, what I did that I got a good friend. We knew each other since childhood...and we both were very good friends, we helped each other. You always describe me as sweet and kind, and I also think you are kind. What I liked about you was, that you can make anyone happy, even if it meant you have to sacrifice yourself... Julia never became angry on me, instead, she blamed herself... So many times, I came in fights and you were the only one... who helped me to fight! You were the kindest person, I have ever met. We were also known as 'the best duo' and all were very jealous of us! We also don't hate each other! But not gonna lie, you helped me a lot then I do... you helped me in writing my assignments and projects and always cared about others, and didn't bother about yourself... I still remember one day you told me, 'Winston do you know? Yesterday, I was so worried about whether you completed the assignment or not!' you were the weirdest! One day, it happened that you got scolded because of me. I went to play badminton, and you! You wrote my notes without asking me! And because of that, you didn't get time to write your notes and got scolded for not completing your notes, I still remember... you would risk your life for someone very important to you! I also remembered a thing! You were very good at hiding your sadness... you just showed a smile, even if it's a sad moment or a happy moment... 'I didn't get good marks' I said, and you just smiled and said, "Don't worry! It's okay to get 13/20! I got 10/20' you lied, you got 20/20 but you lied to me just to make me happy because someone got fewer marks from me so I will get less worried... But hey! Not to forget, I am also kind! You always said that 'you always take things to positive only!' and an example is... 'hey! At least I didn't get a bad mark!' I said, and you smiled and agreed... I even defended you, so many people were making fun of you because of your height and I said, 'So? So what is the problem with being short? What have you done by being tall?'. And well, this was about me and you! I will miss you Julia and may you rest in peace, my pal..."

• • •

Winston went to the police station and asked Marie and Martin, "Was Julia murdered?" He asked, "Yes," They said, "Please, do anything and find the murderer! Whatever help do you need, I will try my best to help you all!" Winston said, "Sure Winston, in the future, we would need your help but for now, please take care, we know your heart is broken and you are sad, so for now, please go to your house and rest," Marie said, "Okay mam..." Winston said and went away...

CHAPTER V

Some shreds of evidence in the Park

The Police were investigating in the park, suddenly, a police officer came to Marie and Martin and said, "We have found something! Come with us!" Marie and Martin followed the police officer, they were in a corner of the park, "A Photo?" Marie asked, she took the photo and looked at it... It was Winston! "This is Winston's photo! What is it doing here?" Martin asked, "Look! Below it, it is written '*Kill him*' What does this mean?" Marie asked, "We also found Julia's phone," The police officer said, "Let's take this photo, we can get fingerprints!" Martin said, the police officer took the photo for investigation, Marie checked the phone, "So it's... Julia's phone. Let's see the call history, what? The last call was to the police on 13 August! A month ago!" She said, "It is the day when Julia went missing!" Martin said, "I am going to ask some questions to Julia's family members!" Martin said and went to Julia's house... Martin reached Julia's house, "Welcome Sir!" Julia's mother said, "Hello Miss. Wilde, I have come here to ask some questions, so would you answer it?" Martin asked, "Sure!" Julia's mother replied. "So, do you remember on 13 August, where was Julia?" Martin asked, "Isn't that the day when my daughter went missing?" Julia's mother asked, "Yes" Martin replied, "I think she went to the park for a walk but didn't come," Julia's mother said, "So from here Julia went missing..." Martin said, "Thank you, if you get anything related to the case, then please inform us," Martin said and went away... Martin went to meet Winston, "Let's see how our little buddy is!" Martin said in a jolly voice but when he went to Winston's house, he saw Winston was not paying attention and was lost in his world. Martin was confused, he called Winston, "Winston! Winston! Winston, are you even listening to me?" But Winston didn't answer it... seeing all this, Martin became sad and went away. "Oh, Man! Winston looks so depressed. I am just worried about him" Martin thought. He felt exhausted, "I am thinking to take a break! And what could be the place other than Tes Med!" Martin thought and went to the police station, he told all this to his friends and took a break today, He went to his house and visited his neighbor, Winston. "Winston! I have an offer for you! Would you come with me to Tes Med?" Martin asked, "I would rather be indoors" Winston replied, Martin was speechless. "Okay, buddy. As you wish!" Martin said *and smiled*. After seeing the smile, Winston had a surprising face and stared at Martin. And, Martin went away... He packed his bag and went to the railway station, "When will the train come? Oh! After half an hour! That's fine... Meanwhile, I will call Andrew (Martin's cousin who lives in Tes Med)" Martin tried to call Andrew, "Hello Andrew?" Martin asked, "Yes! What happened?" Andrew replied, "Andrew, can I come to your house?" Martin asked, "Sure bro!" Andrew said politely, "Thanks, bro! See you soon!" Martin said and ended the call. A few minutes later, Martin's train came and he hopped in. A few hours later, he reached Tes Med. He explored the most famous park called *Winslain Park*. He went to Andrew's house and took a nap... After waking up, he freshed himself and did some work on the case. It was 5:30 PM, Martin said to Andrew, "Andrew! Thank you for your hospitality, thank you for letting me take a nap, and for the food, you gave me. So... Can you do a favor for me? I would go back to Kine Med at 6 PM, can you remind me?" Martin asked, "Sure!" Andrew replied. Martin went back to work, he noticed something, "This picture (picture of Winston which was found in the park) has *Julia's fingerprint*! It means Julia has touched this picture. But, this would not make any sense, Julia was trying to kill Winston, NO! That's not possible. *Was Julia a witness?*" He asked himself... Suddenly, Andrew came and said, "Bro! It's going to be 6 PM, look it's already 5:45 PM!" "What!!?? How does this time pass so fast? Martin said and went away. But, he forgot the picture of Winston. At 6:10 PM, Martin's train came and he hopped in. At 7 PM, he reached Kine Med and went to the police station to say the theory but... he realized, he doesn't have the picture and was scared! He took out his phone and saw, *He missed many calls from Andrew*, he called back Andrew, "Martin you forgot some of your files here, I was trying to call, but you didn't pick up my calls!" Andrew said.

CHAPTER VI

"Don't see the first page!"

"I remember..." Martin said, "Are the files important?" Andrew asked, "Yeah... and I need that tomorrow!" Martin said, "But... the next train to Tes Med is at 10 PM! And to Kine Med, it is at 1 AM!" Andrew said, "That's fine to me! I will come to your place" Martin replied, "Okay... and what about the reason why you were not picking up my calls?" Andrew asked, "I was so busy with the work that I put my phone on silent mode and forgot to turn it off in hurry!" Martin said, "Oh... okay bro, bye!" Andrew said and the call ended... Martin told his friends that he have to go back to Tes Med to bring the files. At 9:45 PM, Martin went to the railway station, and when the train came, he went in, and when he reached Tes Med at 11:05 PM, he went to Andrew's house, "Martin, so when you are planning to go back to the railway station?" Andrew asked, "Probably 12:40 AM" Martin asked, "Oh, it's a good time also!" Andrew said. When it was 12:40 AM, Andrew farewelled Martin and Martin went away, after reaching the railway station, he saw a man selling magazines, "It's midnight! But the man is still selling magazines!" Martin said to himself, he called the man and asked a question to the man, "Dear seller, I have a question, why are you selling magazines at this time? You should take a rest at this time!"

"Dear Sir, I appreciated that you asked about me, but I think, I should not say this to you. Anyways, it's also my job to do!" The man said, "Oh, wait... I have seen you somewhere, do I know you?" But the man didn't answer Martin's question and asked, "Sir would you like to take this magazine?" Martin thought for a second and said, "Sure! How much is it?" "It's 100 R Med (Their currency)" The seller said, Martin gave him 100 R Med and purchased the magazine, "Does this man trying to give me some hint? Does he want to say something to me, but not able to?" Martin thought, suddenly someone bumped into him and tried to steal the magazine, but Martin took the magazine from the strange person, but the strange person said, *"Don't see the first page!"* and went away, Martin was confused but was also scared, "What does he mean by 'don't read the first page?' Is there something in it? Should I even see??" Martin was worried. The train came and he went in it... and when he reached Kine Med, he went to his house and took a nap, at 6 AM, he woke up and went to the police station. He told his friends about the incident that happened with him in the railway station, "I am very scared, what does the man mean?" Martin said, "Do you remember that strange person wearing anything or how does he look?" Marie asked, "I remember, *he wore a big coat, in a black color... he hid his face with a handkerchief,*" Martin said, Marie was shocked, "How? This is the same person who bought the pistol from the black market! He also wore the same things!!" Marie said, hearing this, all were shocked, "It's sure! That seller was trying to hide something from us! Something is there in that magazine!!" Martin said, suddenly, a person entered the police station, oh! It is the tea seller, he brought the tea for the police officers. "Wait, were you there in the Tes Med's railway station, because I am sure, I have seen you there, selling magazines," Martin said...

CHAPTER VII

My friend...

"What? But I don't sell magazines, and why would I be in Tes Med?" The tea seller said, *and laughed nervously,* everyone felt it very suspicious and they drank the tea. "Yeah! As we were talking about the magazine, I will bring that right now!" Martin said and went to his house, he saw Winston outside the house, "Winston? What are you doing here?" Winston heard... he remembered a memory,

(flashbacks):-

2 years ago, it was a normal day but not for Julia... Julia was sad because Winston didn't come to school because he was not feeling well. All Julia's friends told her, "Stop thinking about him!! He is just not well, and also, you look sick, so just stop thinking!" They said angrily, but Julia can't do that, "How am I supposed to do that?" Julia asked, her friends sighed and went away... "They don't know how it feels when your 'best friend' is absent. I even thought to take leave too!" Julia thought. The next day, Winston came to the school and Julia was happy, she told him what happened yesterday and how her friends were annoyed with her, "Yeah, they don't know how it feels!" Winston said, "What about your health? How is it?" Julia asked, "It's fine, just having a headache" Winston replied, "Oh..." Julia said. After school, Julia went to the bus stop, while she was going, she saw Winston, *"Winston? What are you doing here?"* Julia asked, "Umm..." Winston was nervous, "you have a headache, you should take rest! And wait, why are you eating these junk foods? You were not allowed to eat these!" Julia said angrily, meanwhile, Winston's friends

were laughing, "Julia... I have to go, bye..." Winston said, "Huh? Fine, bye!" Julia replied...

• • •

Back to present:

"Hello? Winston?" Martin asked, "Uhh... Martin Sir?" Winston said, "Were you in your imaginary world? What are you doing here?" Martin again asked, "Nothing, I thought to take a walk, so... I would get fit" Winston said, "Oh... ok buddy! You were blank for some minutes, what happened to you?" Martin asked, "When you said, 'what are you doing here?' it reminded me of Julia because a couple of years ago, she asked me this same question..." Winston said, "I didn't know that your memory power is so good!" Martin said, and went to his house, took out the magazine, and went to the police station. "Here is the magazine! Now let's see what's on the first page... They opened the magazine and saw a note, all were shocked, "Huh? A note? What is written on it?" Marie asked, "Let me read.." Martin said, and started to read...

"This is not okay! Aaron... He is not my friend whom I know. It feels like someone else is in his place, he also spends most of the time in his basement as his wife, Cecilia told this. I got some bad feelings about him. So, please Martin Sir read this and found about Aaron, my friend. His real name is 'Aaron Forge'. He doesn't do this jobwhich is *selling magazines, newspapers* and I am Darren Forfeiture, yes I am the *tea seller*, you thought I met you in the Tes Med, then it's true... And I was not able to tell you this in person because I am scared if the 'fake Aaron' does something to me, I know it will happen, it's time to say goodbye! Please find the fake Aaron, he is suspicious!" Martin ended reading the note... "We have to find Darren!

Where is he?" Marie shouted and, all started to find him, but he was nowhere to seem, "His shop was near the police station! Did you find him there?" Marie asked, "We tried to find there also... but he was not there!" The police officers said all started to get worried... "We should start finding this 'fake Aaron'. Who he is? Let's find out!" Martin said. Half crew members were searching for Darren and the other half were busy finding information about Aaron. "We should call his wife, Cecilia!" Martin said...

CHAPTER VIII

Who is Aaron Forge?

Marie called Cecilia, "Afternoon, Mrs. Forge" Marie said, "you called me?" She asked, "Don't worry, miss. You are safe here, you have to just answer some of our questions regarding your husband" Marie said, "Okay" Cecilia said, she was very scared. "Feel free to answer!" Marie said. "Miss, have you found any changes in your husband these days?" Marie asked, "Yes... he doesn't talk with me that much compared to the old days," She said, "Does he do his job every day?" the next question came, "He often goes outside, and I was afraid to ask him, why he is was not doing his job..." she answered,

"If Aaron wasn't going outside, he would be indoors, so what does he do indoors?" Marie asked, "I also don't know what he does in his *basement*, he is always in the basement, while in the old days, he rarely went to the basement," Cecilia said, "As Darren wrote in the note, 'he also spends most of the time in his basement. But what does he do there, nobody knows?" Marie thought..." Well, thank you for your answers! Also, can some of our crew members come to the basement, we have to investigate it" Marie said. Suddenly, a crew member came running and said, "WE FOUND A BODY IN THE MIDDLE OF KINE MED AND JEPS MED!!" All were surprised and went there, "Miss, you can go to your house, just be careful or you can go with one of our crew members, "I prefer going with a police officer" Cecilia said, "Okay, I will call someone" Marie said and called a police officer, the police officer went to Cecilia's house, "Can you please investigate the basement?" Cecilia asked, "I would, but I don't have my equipment," The police officer said, "Oh okay," Cecilia said, the police officer went away... Everyone went to the corpse's spot. "Who is he?" Marie asked when they saw the corpse's face, they were shocked... "No way!" Martin said, "HE-HE IS DARREN!!" A crew member shouted...

"How is this possible? In the morning, he was with us, but... now, he is dead?" Martin said, "Isn't that a *coincidence*?" Marie asked, "What is co-incidence?" Everyone asked, "The news of Darren being dead, came when we were going to the basement! Doesn't it sound like *someone was trying to stop us*? As there is something in the basement, but we should not see it?" Marie said, "You are right, Marie!" Martin said, "Half crew members! Investigate the corpse! We should go to the basement!" Martin said, "Yeah, let's go!" Marie said. Half crew members started to investigate the corpse, and others, including Marie and Martin... They reached Aaron's house and met Aaron, "Afternoon Mr. Forge" Martin said, "Good afternoon officers, what happened? Why are you here? Do you have your warrant?" Aaron asked, "Yes, we have our warrant. We have come here to investigate you and your house." Marie said, "Why do you want to see my house?" He asked, "Trying to defend himself? Not here!" Martin thought and smirked, "Your friend, Darren Forfeiture, put a case on you that you are not his friend and someone else," Martin said, and they handcuffed Aaron, "But! Why are you handcuffing me?" Aaron asked, "So that, you don't make any suspicious move!" Marie said. Martin and some crew members went towards the basement, "Ugh! A disgusting smell is coming from here!" A crew member

said to Martin, they went inside it, and saw... something shocking, "WHAT THE-!!!!" They screamed, "HOW IS

THIS POSSIBLE!??? ANOTHER DEAD BODY!!" They screamed, the police officers heard this and were shocked. The officers came to the basement, some were blank, some were shocked and some were disgusted... "I heard you saw a dead body! Is it true??" Marie asked, Martin noded, Marie was shocked. Then, the police took out the dead body, Cecilia was shocked, "This can't be true!! It-it is Aaron! If this is Aaron, then who is he??" Cecilia asked, "The 'fake' Aaron, we are going to take him to the police station because he is a suspect," Marie said sadly. Cecilia started to cry and went away...

CHAPTER IX

A serial killer who was a hitman

"So, Mr. Fake Aaron, can you explain, why was there a dead body of the real Aaron?" The police officers asked, "For living like Aaron!" He said, "What's the reason?" They asked, "I needed an identity!" He said, "What's the reason?" They asked, "Because I need to," He said, "This man is not going to, say us the main reason!" Martin said to Marie. "Mr. Fake Aaron, you are not going to give us your real identity so you are going to be in jail as you are a *suspect* for killing the real Aaron..." Martin said, "Fine" Fake Aaron replied. Marie went to Darren's corpse investigation, "Did you find anything?" She asked, "Yes! As usual, this is murder!" The police officer said, "What about the weapon?" Marie asked, "*A knife*," the police officer said, "Was Julia murdered with a knife?" Marie asked, "Yes..." he replied, Marie was surprised, "I think the murderer of Darren and Julia are the same! Try to find the knives used in the murders" Marie said, the police officer started to work in it... Meanwhile, Martin was investigating Aaron's dead body. "So Aaron was murdered? I believe he is, because the Fake Aaron said 'I wanted to take his identity" Martin said, "Yes, I also thought that," Another police officer said, "Oh! The results have come, let's go, he said. They went and grabbed the results, "As excepted... another murder!" Martin said, "I knew it! Now we have to just find clues to know who is the murderer!" The officer said and Martin agreed with him..."Was he murdered with a knife?" Martin asked, "Yes..." The officer replied, "That's very strange... Marie told me Julia and Darren were also murdered with a knife!"

Martin said, "Either it's a coincidence or these 3 murders are connecting something!" The officer said, "And when did the murder occur?" Martin asked, "By seeing the corpse, probably 1 week ago..." He replied, "It means this Fake Aaron took Real Aaron's identity a week ago?" Martin asked, "Yes" He replied. Meanwhile... Marie's crew found out the knives used in both the murders... They were shocked, the knives were the same! "It's sure! Darren and Julia's murderer is the same!! We have to tell this to everyone!" Marie said, she called Martin and told them everything, they were also shocked... "We also have found something! Aaron was also murdered with a knife!!" Martin said, "Then try to find the knife used, if it is the same as these two, then it's sure a *serial killer* killed all the three!" Marie said. Martin and his crew started to find the knife. After few hours later, they found the knife and... *it's the same knife as the knives used for Julia and Darren!!* All were shocked, Martin immediately called Marie and told the news, "I knew it! Let's meet at the police station" Marie said, everyone went to the police station, "So... Julia, Darren, and Aaron's murderer is the same... But how can we find the serial killer?" Marie asked, "We should try to examine the knife we found in the park, the place where Julia's corpse was found!" Martin said, "Okay!" Marie replied they all took the knife used to kill Julia and examined the knife, after doing some experiment, they found two fingerprints, one belonged to Julia and the other... belonged to someone else. After some research, they found who the fingerprints belonged to...Cole Vain, a hitman.

"Now this makes sense... So a hitman killed all the three, but why?" Martin asked, "Because its his job! Someone gave him money to do all these, Cole probably didn't have any intentions!" Marie said, "Let's try to find his house," Martin said, and they tried to find his house and when they found out, they went there. "He lives in Nas Med..." Marie said. They reached Cole's house and raided it! "This is Police! We have come here to find Cole, Cole comes out and asked, "What's happening!!?? Police??" He shouted, "Cole... you are under arrest for killing 3 people, now tell us for whom you did?" Marie said, "I am okay with going to Jail but, should I tell you the reason... I am very scared!" Cole said, "Why are you scared?" Martin asked, "No no no!! I am going to die! I can say, I didn't kill Winston's Family, he killed them because he wanted to take revenge!" Cole said, "Who killed Winston's family?" "Do-Donald! He wanted to take his brother, Jim's revenge!" Cole said, "Do you mean the thief, Jim Foul?" Martin asked, Cole, nodded, suddenly someone shot Cole, "WHAT!!!??" No one was able to see the person who shot!" All were shocked, Cole was dead...

CHAPTER X

Everything is going to End...

Cole's corpse was taken away, "That was unexpected!" Marie said, "Yeah... Also, I am going to meet Winston, try to find out about Donald!" Martin said, "Sure!" Marie said. Martin went to Winston's house, "Winston! Winston! I have news for you!" Martin said, "What news do you have Sir Martin?" Winston asked, "We found Julia's murderer!" Martin said, "REALLY?? WHO IS IT!!??" Winston asked and tears dropped from his eye, "Aww, Winston don't cry, you should be happy" Martin said, "No sir, this is the tears of joy!" "Oh... Well, the killer was a hitman hired by someone" Martin said, "WHAT? A hitman?" Winston was confused, "Yes... but today he died. We are trying to find who hired him, don't worry! Keep hopes!" Martin said, "Yes!" Winston said and smiled. Martin went back to the police station, "Did you find anything about Donald?" He asked, "Yes, we found a lot! *Donald Foul, brother of a thief* named Jim Foul which Cole was talking about.

• • •

So, a few years ago, Jim stole money from Winston's family and got caught because Winston's father, Paul Monet caught Jim. Jim was also a professional thief! So, after taking him to the court, he was sentenced to 20 years! But he somehow escaped and then again started stealing, and then again Paul caught him! That was a really big coincidence!! This time, when he took Jim to the court, Jim was sentenced to death!! So that he would not roam around the city and steal. After executing Jim, Donald heard this news, he was sad as his brother died, he was very angry at Paul and decided to kill his family, so a few years later, he killed them all, but as Winston was lost and was not in the house, he was not killed! So, that's why he hired Cole to kill Winston! Because he knew that he will get caught... And as you had a theory that Julia was a witness, well, that's true! We found some footage cameras now, and Julia and Cole bumped each other, because of it, the picture of Winston fell from Cole's bag, and he didn't notice it. Julia took the picture, after seeing 'kill him' she was scared and called the police but Cole saw her, so he didn't wanted to get caught, he killed Julia so that no one can know about him... For me, it's more like a sacrifice! Darren was dead because he tried to expose the fake Aaron, and I think the Fake Aaron was the one, who hired Cole!" Marie said. "We should ask him!" Martin said, "Do you think he will say?" Marie asked, "Let's try! I have an idea" Martin said,

• • •

they went to Fake Aaron's room, but they didn't find the Fake Aaron... "Wait, what? Where did the Fake Aaron go? Why he is not here??" Martin asked, "No way! He escaped! How is this possible??" Marie asked, they were surprised, they told all the police officers, that *Fake Aaron has escaped!* All started to find him after a few hours later, they found a body near Jeps Med. All police officers went there, "So now who is dead?" Marie asked, Martin was shocked after seeing the corpse's body... "No- NO WAY!! HE IS FAKE AARON!!" He shouted, "WHAT!!??" Marie asked. *The dead body was Fake Aaron's...* "Look! There are some bullets!" Martin said, "These are sniper bullets... Wait, these bullets are familiar!" Marie said. They took the bullets with them and the body was taken away... After some examining, the police officers realized it was the same bullet-model used to shoot Cole! "Does it means, the person who killed Cole has also killed the Fake Aaron?" Martin asked, "Yes..." Marie replied. "What is the sniper model?" Martin asked, "**AW50**" Marie replied, "Should we find where does this sniper get as we did before?" Martin asked, "I think, we should... but we also have to find who the fake Aaron really was! His real identity!" Marie said, "Then, let's divide and try to do both the tasks!" Martin said.

Half crew members started to find where does the sniper get and the other half started to find Fake Aaron's real identity. "Marie, I think we should investigate Cole's house, what if we get some clues?" Martin said, "Good idea..." Marie said, and they went to Cole's house. After some investigating, they found some notes, "Look! This note says, *'meet him at Rie Med'* and an address is given, should we go there?" Marie asked, "Yeah we will, after a few minutes..." Martin said. They investigated more, but they didn't find anything interesting. So, they went to the address. It was someone's house, "This house looks abandoned, anyone lives here?" A police officer asked, "The lights are off, and it seems... it's an abandoned house" Marie said, They went inside the house by breaking the door. Everything seems okay until they realized whose house it was... *They saw pictures of Jim and Donald* and all were surprised, "This is Donald's house!" They said and started to investigate the house, and found many pictures of some men, but only (Real) Aaron's picture had a circle! "What does this mean? Why does Aaron's picture is circled?" Martin asked, "Look down!! Something is written 'new identity' what does this mean??" A police officer asked, "I think... it means *Aaron is Donald's new identity! It means Fake Aaron is Donald,* So... it means the person's corpse we found today was... Donald's! *Donald is dead!!*" Marie said, And they went to the police station... "Martin, We also found out who killed Cole, but we don't know his identity. The person who killed Cole is Donald!" "How do you know that Donald killed Cole?" Martin asked, "I remembered from where did the bullets came from, I also took the bullets with me. After some examining, I found out, it was from a Sniper! So, from which building did the bullets come, I took some camera footage of the building and found out, a sniper was there! After some research, we knew that he was hired by Donald. And that's how I knew!!" Marie said. "So, it means Cole and Donald were killed by a sniper, but why did Donald's sniper kill him?" Martin asked, "I don't know" Marie replied. Meanwhile, the other crew found out about the sniper, his name is Ivan Conway, he killed Cole and Donald. A police officer came to Marie and Martin, "We found the sniper!" He said, "That's good!" Marie said, and some police officers were bringing Ivan. "He surrenders himself!" The police officer said, "What happened, how did you find him, can you tell us?" Martin asked, "Sure... We went to Nas Med and asked about the sniper, and the seller told us about the buyer, Ivan. We raided his house and he surrender himself, we asked why did he kill Donald, and he said, 'Donald was going to tell about me, I was scared if I got caught so I killed him, but now, I am feeling ashamed for my actions so I surrender!' and about Cole, well... Donald told him to because Cole was going, to tell the truth about him" The police officer said, "Oh... well, looks like this case is finished, right?" Martin asked, "Yes! We found who is Winston's family and best friend's murderer, the fake Aaron, *Donald was behind all these!*" Marie said, "Now go to Winston's house and tell him! He will be very happy,"

Marie said, Martin went to Winston's house and said, "We found how and why Julia died, we also found your family's murderer!" And Martin told why was Julia murdered and his family's murderer... "Thank you so much!! Now I finally knew who did all these!" Winston said and started to cry... "I am sorry, my tears are not stopping," Winston said. Martin smiled and went away...

CHAPTER XI

Old Memories...

Martin went to the police station, "So what did Winston say?" Marie asked, "He was crying, he was very happy! Martin said, "Okay..." Marie said and smiled. Winston saw Julia's picture and his family members and said, "Look! The murderer, he is caught but... he is dead. I am very happy that he is dead! But how Donald took revenge on dad was cruel, *The Cruel Revenge*" Winston said...

After 16 years later, Winston was a 30-year-old man. He went to his friend, Oscar Crony's house. "Hello Mate!" Winston said, "Winston!? What happen?" Oscar asked, "Nothing, just wanted to visit you and my nephew and niece!" Winston said, "Oh. Come inside..." Oscar said, "Hello!!" Winston said to his nephew and niece, "Yay!! Uncle Winston!" Dora said, Oscar's daughter. "Uncle we want to listen to some stories, our father is not saying us!" Carl said [Oscar's son] said. "Okay! It's a very years ago! Like 17 years ago!" Winston said, "Oh!" They were surprised, "It is about a kind girl, let's name the story *Your kindness will never end...*

So, a girl named Julia was very kind. One day, she was waiting for her friend, called Winston, he was doing some work, Julia would have gone away leaving him but she didn't! Julia waited for 10 minutes, and at last, Winston came and saw Julia, he said, "You waited for me! Thank you!" "It's nothing to say Thank you!" Julia replied, "And that's why you are my best friend!" Winston said, Julia was confused, "You always care about me, but my other friends! They don't even do that! That's why you are the best!" Winston said, and Julia smiled... But, suddenly that smile turned into a sad face, Winston asked her, "What happened?" "Remember my friends! They broke friendship with me!" Julia said, hearing this, Winston was happy. "Why are you happy?" Julia asked, "I knew they will do this! Also, they are very toxic, that's why you need only 1 friend and that's me!! But, for some reason, they hate our friendship..." Winston said, "Yeah, they broke the friendship because of you, I think they hate you!" Julia said, "Of course! Why does everyone hate me?" "Because of your grumpiness!" Julia said and laughed, "What! No!" Winston said... Those good old memories!

So, This story shows Julia and Winston's kindness! And that's why you two also should be like them!" Winston said, "But Uncle, you are the Winston in the story, right?" Dora asked, "Yes!" Winston replied, "Oh... but Aunt Julia is not with us," Carl said, "Yes..." Winston said in a sad tone. "Forget it! So how was the story??" Winston asked, "Very nice!! Aunt Julia's friends were very bad!! Why did they hate you, that's very bad!!" They said, "Yes, that's why you should stay away from them!" Winston said. "Oh! It's time to go, bye children!!" Winston said and went away. "BYE!! UNCLE WINSTON!!" The children said...

THE END

• • •

Characters And Their Names

Marie Sanders- A police officer

Winston Monet- His family was missing and he complained about it to the police

Martin Branson- A police officer

Julia Wilde- Winston's best friend

June Wilde- Julia's elder sister

Steven Monet- Winston's cousin

Micheal Monet- Winston's younger brother

Andrew Branson- Martin's cousin

Aaron Forge- the villain took his identity and lived like him

Cecilia Forge- Aaron's wife

Darren Forfeiture- A tea seller and Aaron's friend, he found suspicious about his friend, so he complained it to the police

Cole Vain- A hitman hired by the villain

Jim Foul- a professional thief

Donald Foul- Jim's brother and took his revenge

Paul Monet- Winston's Father

Oscar Crony- Winston's Friend

Dora Crony- Oscar's daughter

Carl Crony- Oscar's son

Ivan Conway- A sniper hired by the villan

• • •

Places Mentioned In The Story (they Are Not Related To The Real-life)

Jeps Med- Place where Winston's relatives live

Kine Med-Place where Winston live

Las Med- Place where Winston's family members' corpses were found

Nas Med- Place where the police officers found a black market, Cole live here

Kine Med Forest- Place where the Monet family went on a trip

Tes Med- Place where Martin went to so he could take a break

Winslain Park- The most famous Park in Tes Med

Tes Med's railway station- Place where Martin found a strange magazine

Middle of Kine Med and Jeps Med- Place where Darren's corpse was found

• • •